SUE COE

PIT'S LETTER

My dearest sister,

It grieves me to inform you that from our litter of six you are now the lone survivor. Knowing you still exist, and that you are safe, makes my loneliness bearable.

    I hid out after Mother died and they took you away. I don't know how long I lived on the street.

    Then, the miracle! A young boy named Pat Watson found me. He brought me home and called me Pit. I had a human that loved me and a warm place with food.

I went everywhere with my human. I was a Velcro dog. We were never separated. I never wanted to be alone again. I guarded him when he slept. I followed him to school and waited outside all day for him.

After school, we would go into the woods with the other kids, and they would get into mischief. The boys would attract moths to a flame and then pull their wings off. They would drop the writhing, wingless bodies down the girls' clothes.

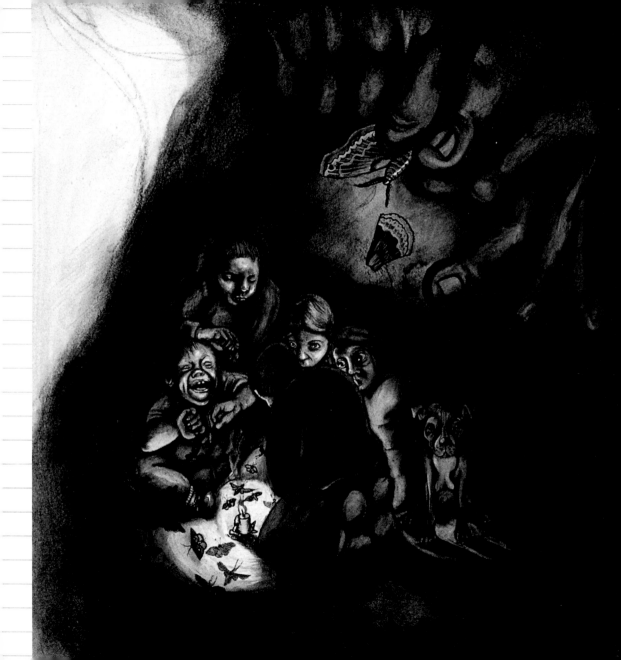

Still, our adventures were magical. We would play and play and never want to go home. We would stay outside until after dark. To Pat, I was Lassie and Rin Tin Tin. I saved him and he saved me, in imaginary adventures again and again.

But human packs are not like dog packs. In the dog world, each dog belongs; even the weakest ones share in the protection of the pack. Humans are different. They don't work together for the good of all. The strong ones bully those who are not as strong; the bullied find others with even less power, to bully. It makes the bullies feel strong.

Pat got a good feeling by acting strong with his friends, only acting strong meant being a bully, just like his father. My human and his gang were in a drug store, and they terrorized a homeless woman by spraying her with air freshener.

One night they captured a young woman with the mind of a child, who had been thrown out of her pack. They knew she could never tell on them. When they were finished, one of the boys gave her his penknife.

The gang wanted to see me fight other pit bulls, but I was never trained to fight my brothers and sisters. Pat didn't have the heart to sew razor-blades under my skin or pour gunpowder into my open wounds to make me fierce.

I would look into the mad eyes of the dog fighters, and they would be dead.

Pat showed me photographs in science magazines of dogs with two heads and monkeys tied into chairs with the tops of their skulls sawed off. He grew excited and passionate when he thought about trying to do things no one had ever done before. I believe it was his biology class that set him on the path that would change his life and mine.

The students had to cut up frogs. My Pat always got good grades in science, and then the girl who always got the highest marks refused to cut up her frog. She said it wasn't necessary—computer models existed. The teacher tried to force her, but she refused.

So Pat came home with the science prize, and his father was proud of him. This was one time when he didn't call Pat a loser.

That night, Pat made me sleep on the floor, instead of at the foot of his bed.

Pat dreamed he would be a scientist and create new life-forms, cure cancer, make the covers of *Time* and *Newsweek,* win the Nobel prize. His life story would be movie meat! I had a feeling of doom.

Pat could prove his destiny was the right course. It said so in the Bible. "God gave you dominion over all living things.... (T)he fear of you, the dread of you, shall be on every beast of the earth." For us, dearest sister, if we believed in their God the Devil would look like a human being.

Pat and his father would go hunting. Mr. Watson said it was the only activity left that a father and son could enjoy together. Mr. Watson said that if Pat had been a girl, he would go to the mall with his mother. Pat hated hunting but did not want to disappoint his father. The noise of the semiautomatic weapons and the stench of beer filled the woods.

One day, Mr. Watson and his brother took us hunting. By 10 AM, they were drunk and angry: they had only killed a small doe. Mr. Watson started to scream and shout at Pat for being a sissy like his mother and for not having a real hunting dog.

And then he raised his fist and was going to strike my friend. In that moment, I became a different dog—the fur on my back rose and I bared my teeth. Growling, I faced Mr. Watson—for the first time my eyes looked directly into his. I would protect my master, no matter what.

I smelled Mr. Watson's fear. He lowered his fists and backed away. I started to wag my tail, proud that I had protected my Pat and to show that all was forgiven. I even tried to lick Mr. Watson's hand. But Pat didn't look at me. Instead, he got into the back of the truck. I tried to follow but his father slammed the door, and they drove away.

The breath stopped in my throat: I thought my heart would burst. In the small space of hope, I thought it was a trick. They would stop the truck—

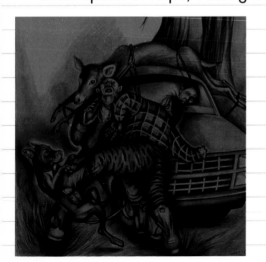

I would bound in, and Pat would hug me. I ran and ran, the truck growing smaller and smaller. The dead deer tied to the roof bounced up and down, her sad eyes watching me. The last thing I saw was the sobbing face of my only friend as he watched me disappear into a speck, and then no more.

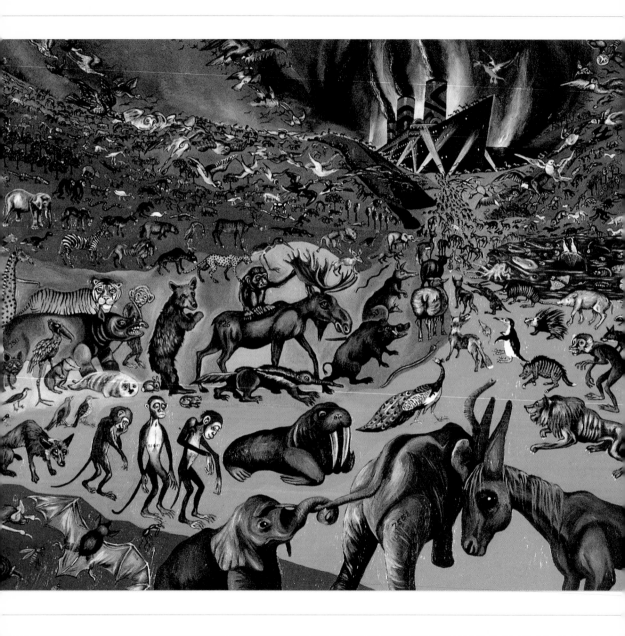

Coyote bodies hung from the fences beside the road.

    I walked through past and future, rotten with killing, searching for some hope. Animals that were never meant to be, man-made monsters, sprouted like strange flowers from a singed landscape; lethal viruses multiplied and consumed the over-crowded populations; air, water, earth poisoned; all the rich variety of life and history rendered null, fit only to be ground into profit. Separated from the tree of wisdom, knowledge partners cruelty. Goodness flees.

    But I was just a dog, and now a dog with no one, my bark muted, my fangs blunted, my vision simple.

Sister, I was captured, muzzled, and thrown into a steel cage in a steel room. There were lines and lines of cages, stacked three deep, containing thousands of us. The noise of barking and howling was deafening. On each cage was a justification for why we were there: owner allergic; owner had baby; owner had to move; owner can't afford; or dog found on highway; dog too aggressive; dog too passive; dog soils the house; dog sheds. The list was endless. My neighbor told me that her owner was returning for her shortly, but I could read the code on her door: *Destroy*. My neighbor on the other side had previously been adopted and was so happy that he urinated on the carpet. He was returned to the pound. He too had the destroy code. I couldn't see what was on my cage,

but I assumed it was the same. I was unadoptable—an undesirable breed, no longer a puppy, not a golden color. Eventually, I knew the deep shame of soiling my own cage. No human came to take us out since it was a holiday weekend.

We stood in line for death and watched the electrocutions and poison injections. Some dogs were shivering and crying, trying to tell the executioners that it was all a mistake—*our* humans are coming for us, we even imagined we could hear them at the reception desk. I tried to think about when I was Pat's Rin Tin Tin.

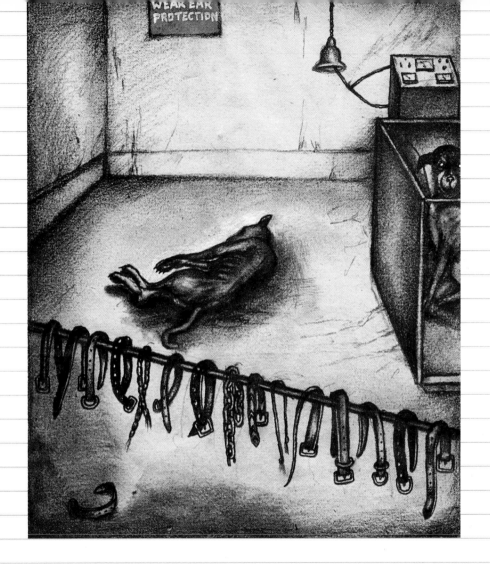

At that moment, a human trader in animal lives appeared. Certain dogs on death row caught his eye. He chose me. I was taken past all that remained of the abandoned: their collars.

"You are found guilty of being an animal — your sentence is torture in a lab until death"

What was our crime? We were guilty of being animals and our sentence was life in a laboratory until death.

I was driven to Eden Technologies Ltd. (official motto: GETTING IT RIGHT FROM THE START).

But as I entered, my heart leapt for pure joy! I caught my master's scent! He had become one of many Eden Tech scientists working on a defense department project to find a cure for empathy. Eden knew that by isolating the gene for empathy their profits would be counted in the billions of dollars.

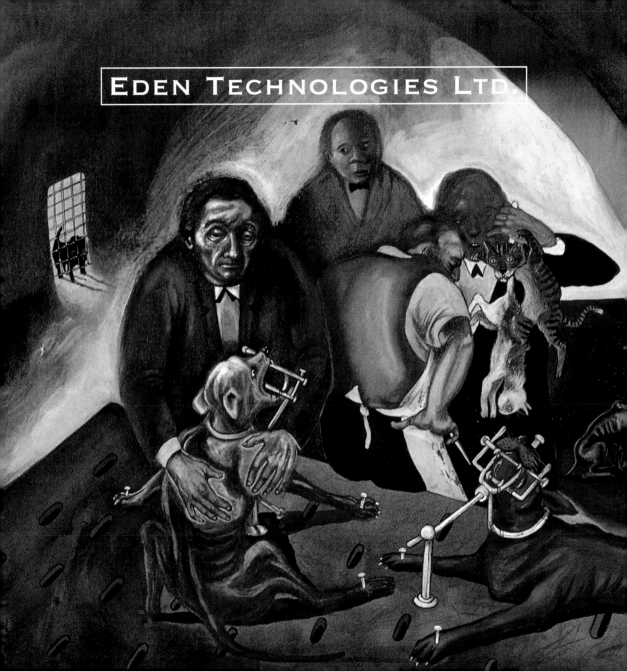

Thousands of us were used in this research. The humans were amazed that I had managed to stay alive after eight experiments. But I refused to die until I saw Pat. All the humans who worked at Eden were great artists of vivisection. It was the policy of Eden Technologies Ltd. to operate on an animal over and over until it died. It was a budget-conscious choice.

The night I first glimpsed Pat, he was asleep after cleaning out the lab. I whimpered to him to awaken, but my vocal chords had been cut. Eden was in a residential district, and the neighbors had complained about our whines and cries.

The monkeys in the lab had the misfortune to be enough like humans to be experimented on, but not enough like humans to have any rights. They were the "lower primates" and I was "man's best friend." We were not sophisticated enough to wage wars of genocide.

Eden gained permission to test on human prisoners. As it had stock in the prison industry this was not difficult. A brief debate ensued: was it ethical to use humans? But labs already used fetal tissue. The genie was out of the bottle once Congress authorized gene patents.

The empathy gene proved elusive. Some were reminded of experiments from long ago—cutting open healthy and alert dogs in search of their souls. I didn't know it then, but Pat, too, had started to question the authorities.

Pat went through a haze of days as he went about his tasks. There was an accident. A small scratch from one monkey pierced his rubber glove, nothing serious, just a graze. Infection set in. Pat's colleagues were very concerned. It could have happened to them.

I was used up, unfit for further experimentation, and had been left on the floor. I dragged myself over to a blinded cat and a dog with an exposed spine. I licked their faces to give them comfort. I crossed my heart and hoped to die. I could not wait any longer for Pat to see me.

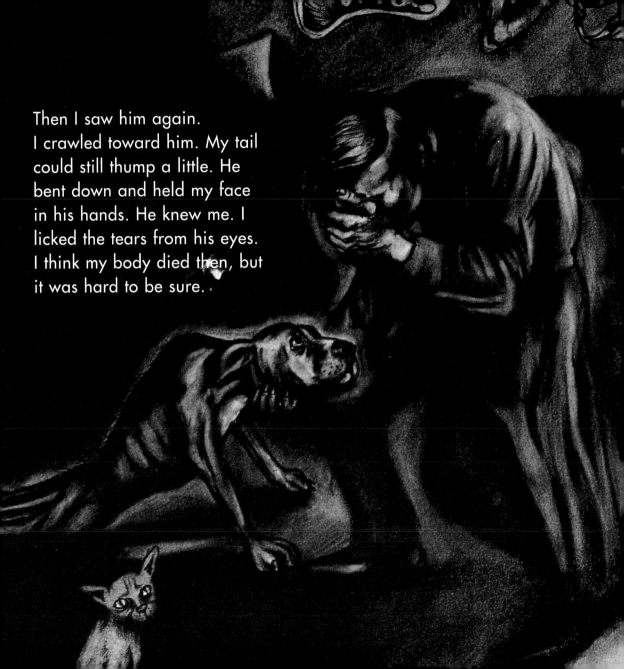

Then I saw him again.
I crawled toward him. My tail
could still thump a little. He
bent down and held my face
in his hands. He knew me. I
licked the tears from his eyes.
I think my body died then, but
it was hard to be sure.

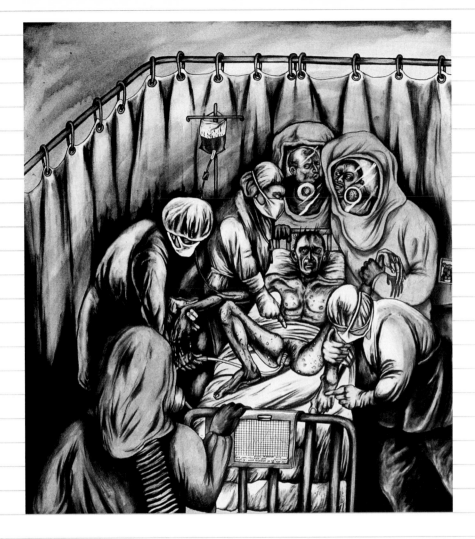

Pat started to die. The owners of Eden Technologies came to visit, dressed in HazMat suits. They paid his hospice fees, although they did not provide health insurance for their employees, and they funded a study on the pathology of his infection.

In Pat's fevered state, he imagined all the animals he had cut open doing the same to him and feasting on his heart. But he knew it was really his colleagues. Their experiment on him had been a success.

In his last days at the hospice, no one came to visit us, except a volunteer who brought with her a rainbow of creatures to give us comfort. Pat brightened and thought he recognized me in the puppy she gave him to hold. He could feel my weight at the end of the bed, but could not see me. The other animals could see me and sang their greetings.

We are together now. I can watch over him and look into the beautiful night and watch the moths fly into the moon. That ends my letter, dearest sister. Do not pity me or have hatred for humans. We can change, we are all brothers and sisters, in fur, fin, skin, and feather.

All my ghostly love, Pit

This book is dedicated to the rescued:
Lucy, Hilda, Spike, Pencil, KJ, Blacky,
Mole, Mouser, Wiggy, Muffin, Spaz,
Honey, Dicklings, Sooty, Ted, Max, Tigger,
Hope, Lassie, Midnight, Little Old Boy,
Tullie, Portia, Kitty, Sam, Samantha,
Sparky, Precious, Hyena, Midnight,
Bobby Cat, Katy, Gretchen, and Clyde.

© 2000 by Sue Coe

Published in the United States by
Four Walls Eight Windows
39 West 14th Street, room 503
New York, NY 10011
http://www.fourwallseightwindows.com

U.K. offices:
Four Walls Eight Windows/Turnaround
Unit 3 Olympia Trading Estate
Coburg Road, Wood Green
London N22 6TZ

First printing May 2000

Library of Congress Cataloguing-in-Publication Data:

Coe, Sue, 1951-
    Pit's letter/Sue Coe.
        p.cm.
    ISBN: 1-56858-163-7 (alk. paper)
        1. Pit bull terriers--Fiction. 2. Human-animal relationships--
    Fiction. 3. Animal welfare--Fiction. 4. Dogs--Fiction. I. Title.

PR6053.027 P58 2000
823'.914--dc21   00-024391

Designed and typeset by Anne Galperin
Sue Coe's artwork photographed by The Soho Photographer
Endpapers are Happy Dog by Sue Coe

Printed in the United States
10 9 8 7 6 5 4 3 2 1